"Good things start with
good ideas." —Linus

Library of Congress Control Number 2014947582
ISBN 978-1-62157-257-2

Published in the United States by
Little Patriot Press
An imprint of Regnery Publishing
A Salem Communications Company
300 New Jersey Ave NW
Washington, DC 20001
www.RegneryKids.com
www.Peanuts.com

Manufactured in the United States of America
10 9 8 7 6 5 4 3 2 1

Books are available in quantity for promotional or premium use. For information on discounts and terms, please visit our website: www.Regnery.com.

Distributed to the trade by
Perseus Distribution
250 West 57th Street
New York, NY 10107

What's the Big Idea, Charlie Brown?

Peanuts created by Charles M. Schulz

Written by Diane Lindsey Reeves and Cheryl Shaw Barnes

Illustrated by Tom Brannon

Little Patriot Press

Big Idea Day started with an idea.

Lucy wanted to have a party. Linus and Sally wanted to celebrate the great inventors they had been learning about in school. Marcie wanted posters. Peppermint Patty wanted prizes. Schroeder wanted—what else?—music. Woodstock insisted on treats.

Finally, it was settled: Saturday was declared Big Idea Day.

Everyone would celebrate big ideas with posters, prizes, music, and treats. The person who found the best big idea would win a blue ribbon.

"Good things start with good ideas," Linus explained to Sally.

Everyone was so excited. They all headed off to find
big ideas that had made the world a better place.

Everyone except Charlie Brown. He wasn't quite sure
what to do. What kind of ideas changed the world?
Who in the world had ideas that big?

"Good grief!" he moaned. "Where am I going to
find a big idea?"

Charlie Brown headed home. An airplane soared in the sky
as he crossed the street at a traffic light. Cars whizzed by.

The telephone at the phone booth rang and rang, but Charlie Brown was so busy worrying that he didn't hear it. He didn't even notice that the baseball glove he'd been wanting was on sale at the corner store.

Grumble, moan, sigh…Charlie Brown muttered all the way home.

Charlie Brown was still worrying when he picked up the telephone to call Linus.

Brriinng, brriinng, brriinng...

Linus answered the phone, but before he said hello—

Aha!

Inspiration struck!

"I have a big idea," Linus said to himself.

"Hello? Linus? Hello?" Charlie Brown called from the other end of the line.

But there was no answer. Linus dropped the phone and ran off to gather his art supplies.

When Lucy came home, she found Linus in the living room. He was busy working on his big idea poster.

"How about a little light in here?" she chided.

Lucy flipped the light on.
Then she switched the light off.

Then on again.

Aha!

"I have the biggest idea of all!" she gloated.

The next morning Lucy couldn't wait to tell Schroeder. As usual, Schroeder was playing the piano.

Lucy tried to get his attention. First, she whispered in a sing-songy voice, "I have a big idea."

Schroeder didn't respond.

Finally, she climbed on top of Schroeder's piano, got right in his face, and said, "My big idea is so big I'm going to win the blue ribbon tomorrow."

"Oh yeah?" Schroeder finally answered. "I have a big idea too."

"Really?" Lucy leaned in even closer. "What is it?" she asked.

KERPLUNK!

"Get lost!" he said. "Can't you see I'm composing the Big Idea Concerto?"

Lucy passed Charlie Brown on her way back home.

"Hey, Charlie Brown," she said. "Do you have a big idea yet? Tomorrow is Big Idea Day, you know."

"Good grief," said Charlie Brown.

Peppermint Patty was on her way home from baseball practice, loaded down with gear.

"Hi, Chuck!" she called out to her friend. Charlie Brown didn't hear her. She waved her hand to get his attention, and

CRASH!

Balls, bats, and mitts went everywhere.

Peppermint Patty bent down to pick them up. She heard a noise behind her.

"What's up with that funny-looking kid?" she wondered.

Beep! Beep!

Peppermint Patty looked to see who was honking their horn at her.

"Marcie!" she called. "Am I glad to see you!"

Peppermint Patty shoved her heavy equipment bag into the backseat. She climbed into the car and let out a sigh of relief.

"Whew," she said. "Wheels move this stuff a lot better than feet."

Hmmm…

The wheels started turning in Peppermint Patty's head.

Aha!

Of course! That's it!

Peppermint Patty had a big idea.

The next morning Charlie Brown came downstairs for breakfast.
He found Sally standing at the kitchen table with a big bowl. Lots
of ingredients were spread in front of her.

"What are you doing?" Charlie Brown asked.

"I'm mixing up a big idea," Sally answered. "Want a taste?"

"Ugh," Charlie Brown groaned. "Even my little sister has a big idea."

Charlie Brown went outside and plopped down under a tree. The pressure was getting to him. A big idea that changed the world? How was he supposed to know?

Snoopy, the Flying Ace, was at it again. But Charlie Brown was too worried to care. He didn't even notice Woodstock giving flying lessons to his friends.

"It's Big Idea Day and I'm the only kid in town who doesn't have a big idea," he moaned.

Charlie Brown was still feeling sorry for himself when Lucy and Linus walked by. They were on their way to the Big Idea Day celebration.

"Wait a minute, Charlie Brown," said Linus. He could tell his friend was miserable. "Don't tell me you still don't have a big idea."

"What a blockhead!" Lucy yelled. "Look up. Look down. Big ideas are all around!"

Charlie Brown looked up. He looked down. He looked all around.

Aha!

Finally.

Charlie Brown had a big idea.

Charlie Brown rushed upstairs to his room. He already knew a lot about this big idea and had just enough time to get his presentation ready.

Things were going really well until he broke his favorite crayon. Then rubbed a hole in the paper with his eraser. And glued the paper to his hand.

It was stuck. He couldn't get it off!

Good grief.

"This will have to do," said Charlie Brown.

Then he dashed down the stairs and out the front door.

Whew! Charlie Brown made it just in time.

The Big Idea Day celebration was in full swing.
Schroeder's Big Idea Concerto was a hit. Lucy,
of course, was his number one fan.

The others were enjoying treats and showing off the big ideas they had discovered.

Then it was time for the competition. Snoopy and Woodstock were the judges, and they took their jobs very seriously.

They decided that Lucy's big idea about the light bulb was
very bright. Linus's telephone idea had a certain ring to it. And
Peppermint Patty's big idea about automobiles had plenty of
zip. Even Charlie Brown's presentation about airplanes got off
the ground…almost.

At last, it was Sally's turn.

Well, now. What do we have here?

And the winner of the blue ribbon is....

The chocolate chip cookie!

What's the Big Idea?

Charlie Brown and his friends discovered big ideas that changed the world. They were so inspired by the people behind those big ideas that they wanted to share their Big Idea Day presentations with you.

What's the Big Idea, Linus?

Telephone

"The inventor...looks upon the world and is
not contented with things as they are.
He wants to improve whatever he sees,
he wants to benefit the world..."

—Alexander Graham Bell

I WONDER WHAT MR. BELL WOULD THINK ABOUT CELL PHONES.

Alexander Graham Bell had a big idea. He wanted to know if people could "talk with electricity." He asked an electrician named Thomas Watson to help him find out. Over time they developed a device that used electric currents to transmit speech from one place to another. The very first words spoken by telephone were "Mr. Watson—come here—I want to see you."

The telephone was Mr. Bell's most famous invention, but it was not his first invention or his last. He had big ideas all of his life and invented many useful things. He was only 12 years old when he invented a de-husking machine for a neighbor's flour mill.

What's the Big Idea, Lucy?

Light Bulb

"Genius is 1 percent inspiration and 99 percent perspiration."

—Thomas Edison

Some people say Thomas Edison was the greatest inventor who ever lived, and I am inclined to agree. How many people do you know that have over 1,000 patents on inventions? He invented a safe and practical light bulb that people could afford to use in their homes. No more messy candles. No more sitting around in the dark. Of course, Edison had to test hundreds of filaments before his idea worked. But he stuck with it until he got it right.

You would think that it would be hard to top that accomplishment. But that is just what Thomas Edison did. Working in his "invention factory" in Menlo Park, New Jersey, Mr. Edison figured out a way to get electricity into homes and businesses so that everyone could use it. I, for one, am very glad Mr. Edison had this big idea.

DID YOU KNOW THAT THOMAS EDISON ALSO INVENTED MOTION PICTURE CAMERAS?

HENRY FORD WOULD BE HAPPY TO KNOW THAT HIS IDEAS KEEP GETTING BETTER.

What's the Big Idea, Peppermint Patty?

Mass-Produced Automobiles

"Whether you think you can, or you think you can't—you're right."

—Henry Ford

Let's get one thing straight. Henry Ford didn't actually invent the automobile. Other people had been tinkering around with the idea of self-propelled vehicles for a long time. Henry Ford wanted to build good cars that lots of people could afford to buy.

At the time, it took 12 hours for teams of workers to make one car. Then Mr. Ford had a big idea. Assembly lines were already used to manufacture everything from steam engines to canned vegetables. Why not cars? Mr. Ford experimented with the idea. He started by using a rope and a winch to move cars along lines of workers. The process got even better when he replaced the ropes with conveyor belts. Now cars could be made in just 93 minutes. That's what I call a huge idea!

THE WRIGHT BROTHERS WERE FIRST IN FLIGHT. SOMEDAY I'D LIKE TO BE FIRST IN LINE.

What's the Big Idea, Charlie Brown?

Airplane

"The airplane stays up because it doesn't have the time to fall."
—Orville Wright

Snoopy likes to pretend to fly even though he is a dog and not a bird. Orville and Wilbur Wright wanted to fly so much that they spent years figuring out how to do it. After lots of trying and failing (boy, do I know a thing or two about that!), they had a big idea that worked. They invented ways for pilots to control airplanes that are still used today. Orville made the first flight at Kitty Hawk, North Carolina, on December 17, 1903! It lasted for 12 seconds. For the first time in history, a flying machine could go where the pilot wanted it to go and, as Wilbur said, "land without wrecking."

After that, flight really took off. Now airplanes and other "flying machines" are flown all over the world and even outer space. Now that's a big idea!

What's the Big Idea, Sally?

Chocolate Chip Cookies

"Measure ingredients accurately and combine carefully."

—Ruth Wakefield

maybe the chocolate chip cookie didn't change the world in the same way that telephones, light bulbs, cars, and planes did. But it sure made the world a much tastier place.

Ruth Wakefield was a trained dietician. She and her husband owned a tourist lodge called the Toll House Inn. One of Mrs. Wakefield's jobs was to make the food. One day she wanted to bake cookies for her guests. She didn't have time to melt the chocolate like the recipe said, so she cut a chocolate bar into pieces and tossed them into the mixing bowl instead. She thought the pieces would melt into the dough to make chocolate cookies. But—surprise!— when she took the first batch out of the oven, she had made something even better.

So, actually, the chocolate chip cookie wasn't a big idea. It was an unexpected surprise. But chocolate chip cookies are still the most popular cookie in America, so I think it is okay to overlook that one little detail. Don't you?

SOME INVENTIONS TASTE BETTER THAN OTHERS.

What's Your Big Idea, Reader?
Describe it!

If you were an inventor, what would you invent?

(Woodstock says to make sure you use a separate piece of paper if this book doesn't belong to you.)

What's Your Big Idea, Reader?
Show it!
Draw a picture of your "big idea" invention.
(Woodstock says to make sure you use a separate piece of paper if this book doesn't belong to you.)